Jasper the Very Lucky Little Kitten

Author: Ken Mackenzie

Illustrator: Genevieve Clarke

Editor and Designer: Chris Stead

Published by: Old Mate Media

www.oldmatemedia.com

First Edition

ISBN 978-1-925638-05-9

Printed by: Createspace
Printed in: United States

Jasper the Very Lucky Little Kitten

Written by: Ken Mackenzie

Illustrations by: Genevieve Clark

Editing and Design: Chris Stead

Our Charity Commitment

Supporting children's hospice SOUTH WEST

Registered Charity No. 1003314

Children's Hospice South West provides care for children who have life-limiting conditions and are not expected to live into adulthood, whilst also supporting their whole family. Old Mate Media is delighted to share that 25% of the profits from the sale of Jasper The Very Lucky Kitten will be donated to the Children's Hospice to help them continue their essential work. Find more information at

www.chsw.org.uk

About The Author

Ken Mackenzie lives in the United Kingdom – Torquay, South Devon to be exact. He is married and is the lucky grandfather to a huge tribe of 11 grandchildren. He loves nothing more than reading stories to the younger generation and taking them on a journey to a brighter, kinder world. He is devoted to the Children's Hospice, and writes his stories in honour of the children no longer with us.

DEDICATED TO

My brother Colin Samual, a lovely man who
always supported my scribblings and stories.
Colin I wish you could have seen me become
a published author.

Mummy cat is lying comfortably in
her basket.

She's watching her baby kitten Jasper play
with a feather.

A big gust of wind had blown it in through
the window.

Jasper was a very pretty kitten with a fluffy white coat and cute black feet.

Plus he had the perfect little black nose, just like a button.

But mummy cat had to watch her kitten all the time.

Jasper was always getting into so much trouble. For instance...

On MONDAY his mummy was napping.

So Jasper crept out of the back door and out into the garden.

His mummy had told him not to go out without her, but he was a naughty little boy

Surely his mummy wouldn't mind if he did it just this once, right?

Jasper had been in the garden only a very short time when things went very bad.

The big black Labrador, Arthur the dog, from next-door spotted him.

Arthur jumped over the fence and chased Jasper round and round the garden.

Jasper was very frightened, but managed to escape into the kitchen.

BECAUSE JASPER WAS A VERY LUCKY BOY

On 𝕿𝖀𝕰𝕾𝕯𝕬𝖄 his mummy was curled up on her favourite blanket

So Jasper ran up the curtains and jumped onto the table next to the goldfish bowl.

With his little black feet, he pulled himself up the bowl

It would be such fun to poke the goldfish!

But with a splash, Jasper toppled right
into the bowl.

And guess what?
He didn't know how to swim!

He began to swallow a lot of water as things
went very bad indeed.

Until the lady of the house spotted him and
yanked him out by his ears.

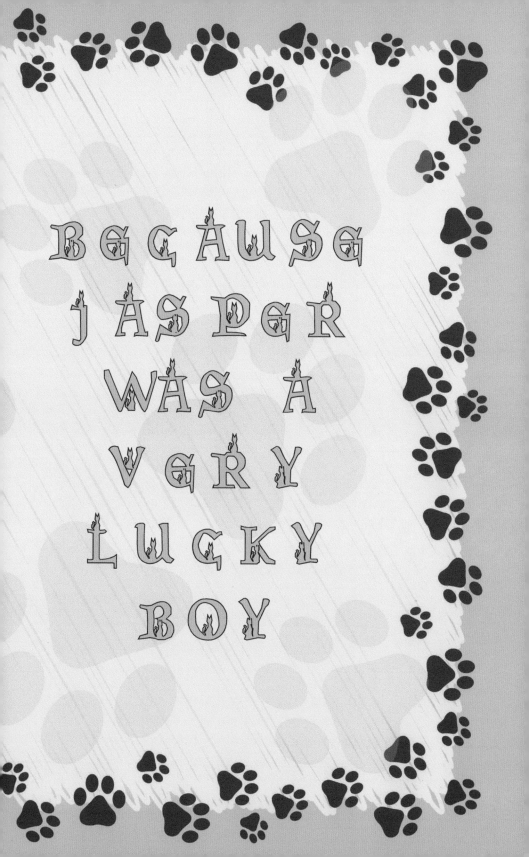

BECAUSE JASPER WAS A VERY LUCKY BOY

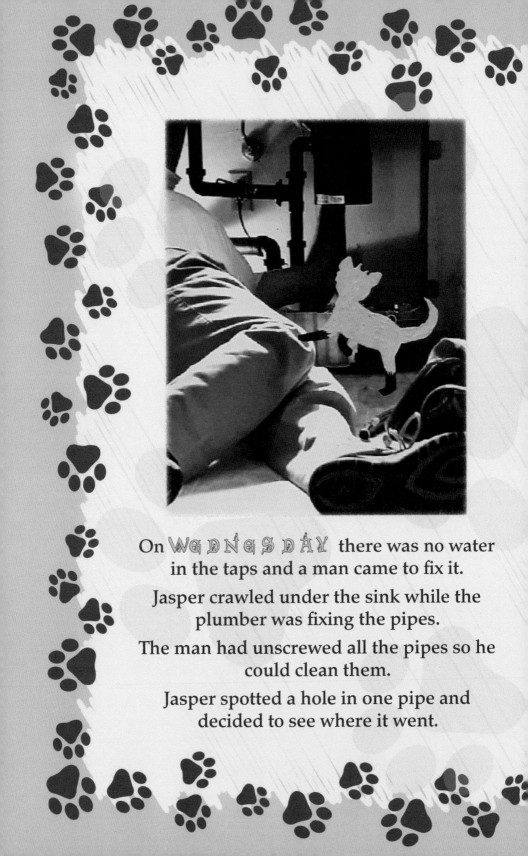

On WEDNESDAY there was no water in the taps and a man came to fix it.

Jasper crawled under the sink while the plumber was fixing the pipes.

The man had unscrewed all the pipes so he could clean them.

Jasper spotted a hole in one pipe and decided to see where it went.

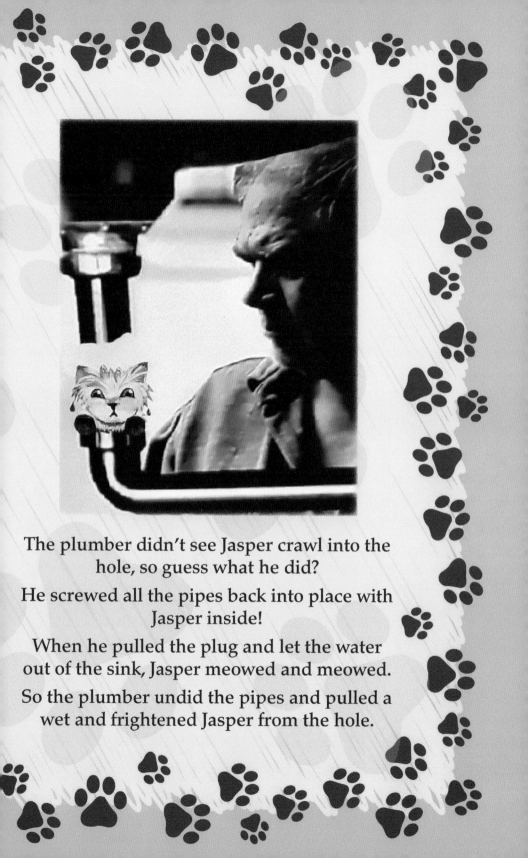

The plumber didn't see Jasper crawl into the hole, so guess what he did?

He screwed all the pipes back into place with Jasper inside!

When he pulled the plug and let the water out of the sink, Jasper meowed and meowed.

So the plumber undid the pipes and pulled a wet and frightened Jasper from the hole.

Because Jasper was a very lucky boy

On ThURSDAY the lady of the house
went to buy groceries.

She put on her coat, picked up her shopping
bag and caught the bus into town.

But guess who was secretly hiding in her
shopping bag?

That's right, it was Jasper.

The lady went to the butcher to get some sausages and you can imagine her fright.

When she opened her bag and little Jasper popped out.

She was not too pleased. The town was a very busy place with a lot of cars and buses.

So before Jasper could get hurt, she stopped shopping and took him all the way home.

BECAUSE
JASPER
WAS A
VERY
LUCKY
BOY

On **FRIDAY** Jasper was in the garden with his mummy when he saw a big black bird up a tree.

Jasper jumped onto the tree and ran up into its branches to say hello.

But the big black bird just flew away.

And when Jasper looked down, he became very frightened, as he was very, very high.

Little Jasper was stuck in a perilous spot.

Luckily the lady of the house called out the fire brigade.

They came with loud sirens and big ladders in order to rescue Jasper.

Mummy cat was very angry, but the fireman thought he was brave and gave him a yummy treat.

BECAUSE
JASPER
WAS A
VERY
LUCKY
BOY

On SATURDAY Jasper woke before anyone else and decided to go for a walk.

He slipped out through the open bedroom window and sat on the window ledge.

It was very quiet and the sun was just starting to rise over the hill tops.

So he stopped to watch the birds flying and listen to them singing in the tree tops.

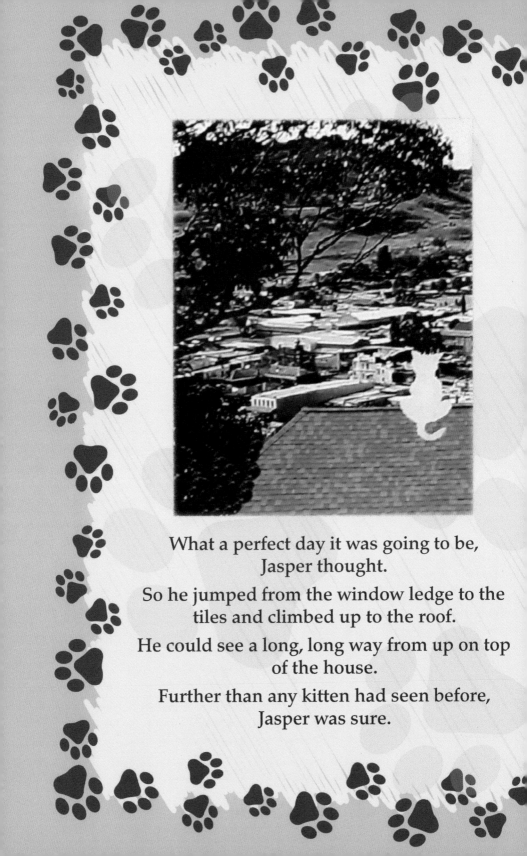

What a perfect day it was going to be,
Jasper thought.

So he jumped from the window ledge to the
tiles and climbed up to the roof.

He could see a long, long way from up on top
of the house.

Further than any kitten had seen before,
Jasper was sure.

After a while Jasper thought he had better go inside before mummy cat woke up.

But his little claws were no match for the hard roof tiles and things quickly went bad.

He teetered, then he wobbled, then he slid right down the roof.

He slid all the way to the gutter and went flying right off the edge.

Poor Jasper was so very afraid as he went rushing for the ground.

Down and down he went.

First past the window, and then past the window ledge.

Until he landed right in a washing basket full of clothes, parked by the clothesline.

BECAUSE
JASPER
WAS A
VERY
LUCKY
BOY

On 𝕊𝕌ℕ𝔻𝔸𝕐 the lady of the house was waiting by the door, peering out the window.

Suddenly, DING! DONG! went the bell and Jasper couldn't contain his excitement.

A man and a little girl walked in and Jasper rubbed up against their legs.

Then the lady of the house pointed at Jasper and said, "this is the one I am selling."

That's when things went bad. Jasper's mum knew she was about to lose her little boy.

He might be a very naughty little cat, but he was her baby and she couldn't lose him.

So mummy cat leapt into the lady's arms and meowed and purred and cried.

That's how the lady of the house could see just how upset it made mummy cat.

"Actually," said the lady of the house,
"I've changed my mind. I will keep this one."

And Jasper leapt from the little girl's hands
to the ground.

Then he ran off with his mummy to hide in
her basket.

"The happiest time of your life is when you
are with your mummy," the lady revealed.

BECAUSE
JASPER
WAS A
VERY
LUCKY
BOY

Tell Us What You Think!

If you enjoyed Jasper's adventures, we would love you to
pop online and leave a review on Amazon or Goodreads.
Reviews help other people find and enjoy independent
books, and help little heroes like Jasper stand out.

To Review on Amazon:

- Put "Jasper the Very Lucky Little Kitten" in the search bar
- Click on the book page
- Scroll down to where it says Customer Reviews
- Click on Write a Customer Review
- Note: You'll need to be logged in to your Amazon account

To Review on Goodreads:

- Put "Jasper the Very Lucky Little Kitten" in the search bar
- Click on the book page that pops up
- Click the box under the cover image, change to "Read"
- A pop-up box will appear for you to leave a review
- Type in your review and leave a star rating, then click save

Thank You

Turn Your Book Dreams Into A Reality

Do you have a story that you tell your kids and grandkids all the time? Are your friends and family always saying, "you should be an author?"

Old Mate Media specialises in helping indie authors self-publish their ideas and own 100% of the copyright. We will walk you down the path to being published.

Visit **www.oldmatemedia.com** for details

Printed in Great Britain
by Amazon

57848667R00020